BUSTER GOES TO THE LIBRARY

WRITTEN BY KATHERINE RAWSON • ILLUSTRATED BY MICHAEL CHESWORTH

CONTENTS

PIONEER VALLEY EDUCATIONAL PRESS, INC.

CHAPTER ONE • BOOKS AND STORIES

It was Saturday morning.

Ricky was walking to the library.

Buster was riding on his shoulder.

"The library is a fun place,"
Ricky told Buster.

"It has thousands of books."

"Books!" squawked Buster.

"Yes," said Ricky, "there are books about everything. And during story hour, the librarian reads us stories."

"Stories!" squawked Buster.

"I have my very own library card,"
said Ricky proudly.
"I can borrow books from the library.
Then I can read the stories to you
at home."

"Books!" squawked Buster. "Stories!"

"You can help me
pick out books, Buster," said Ricky.
"You can listen to the stories
during story hour.
But remember that the library
is a quiet place. At the library,
you have to be quiet."

Be quiet!" squawked Buster.

That's right," said Ricky.
You have to be quiet."

Be quiet!" squawked Buster.
Be quiet!"

Ricky and Buster got to the library and went inside. They saw a big sign by the desk. It said:

Story Hour at 10:00.

"At ten o'clock we can listen to stories," said Ricky.

"Stories!" squawked Buster loudly.

"But it isn't ten o'clock yet," said Ricky. "Let's look at some books."

"Books!" squawked Buster loudly.

"Excuse me," said a voice behind Ricky.
He turned around and saw the librarian.
"Is this your parrot?" she asked.
She was pointing at Buster.

"Yes," said Ricky proudly.
"His name is Buster.
He is a very smart bird. He can talk!"

"I can hear that," said the librarian.

Then she said, "Please tell Buster
that this is the library. At the library
we have to be quiet."

"Be quiet!" squawked Buster loudly.
"Be quiet!"

"Buster," said Ricky,

"remember what I said.
Please be quiet at the library."

"Be quiet!" squawked Buster.

"You will have to take Buster home
if he can't be quiet," said the librarian.

"Be quiet!" squawked Buster.

"But we wanted to go to story hour,"
said Ricky. He looked very sad.

"You can go to story hour,"
said the librarian.
"But Buster will have to wait outside."

Ricky took Buster outside.

He put him on the branch of a tree.

"I'm sorry, Buster," he said.

"Wait for me here.

I will bring you some books

with stories about parrots."

"Books," squawked Buster sadly.

"Stories."

"I will see you soon," said Ricky,

and he went back inside the library.

CHAPTER THREE • BE QUIET!

Ricky saw a long line of people
by the librarian's desk.
They were waiting to check
out their books.

In the other room, Ricky saw
some children. They were sitting
quietly in a circle.
They were waiting for story hour
to begin. Ricky sat down and waited
with them.

After a few minutes, the librarian
came into the room. "I'm sorry, children,"
she said. "I'm very busy helping people.
I will begin story hour soon.
Please wait for me quietly."

The children sat quietly and waited.

They waited and waited.

After a while, they began
to wiggle around.

A girl took a ball out of her pocket.
She threw it in the air. A boy caught it.
He threw the ball to Ricky.
Ricky threw it to another boy.
Soon all the children
were throwing the ball and laughing.
They laughed and laughed.

The librarian stood in the door.
The children didn't see her.
They didn't see the angry look
on her face. They were busy
throwing the ball and laughing.

Suddenly, they heard a loud voice.

"Be quiet!" The children stopped laughing.
They looked at the librarian,
but the librarian wasn't looking at them.
She was looking at the window.
The children looked at the window, too.
Buster sat just outside the window.

"Be quiet!" he squawked again.

The children stared at Buster,

but they didn't say anything.

They were too surprised.

"Buster is right," said the librarian.

"At the library, we have to be quiet.

I can't read stories to noisy children."

The librarian opened the window.
"Buster," she said, "would you like
to listen to stories with us? Quietly?"

"Quietly," squawked Buster very softly.

So Buster sat with the children
and listened to stories.
He listened very quietly
and didn't squawk once
during the whole story hour.